Feeling JEALOUS!

Published in North America by Free Spirit Publishing Inc., Minneapolis, Minnesota, 2017

Library of Congress Cataloging-in-Publication Data
Names: Barnham, Kay, author. | Gordon, Mike, 1948 March 16– illustrator.
Title: Feeling jealous! / written by Kay Barnham ; illustrated by Mike Gordon.
Description: Minneapolis, Minnesota : Free Spirit Publishing Inc., 2017. | Series: Everyday Feelings
Identifiers: LCCN 2017008392| ISBN 9781631982521 (hardcover) | ISBN 1631982524 (hardcover)
Subjects: LCSH: Jealousy in children—Juvenile literature. | Jealousy—Juvenile literature.
Classification: LCC BF723.J4 B37 2017 | DDC 155.4/1248—dc23 LC record available at https://lccn.locgov/2017008392

Free Spirit Publishing does not have control over or assume responsibility for author or third-party websites and their content.

Reading Level Grade 2; Interest Level Ages 5–9; Fountas & Pinnell Guided Reading Level L

10 9 8 7 6 5 4 3 2 1
Printed in China
H13660517

Free Spirit Publishing Inc.
6325 Sandburg Road, Suite 100
Minneapolis, MN 55427-3674
(612) 338-2068
help4kids@freespirit.com
www.freespirit.com

First published in 2017 by Wayland, a division of Hachette Children's Books · London, UK, and Sydney, Australia
Text © Wayland 2017
Illustrations © Mike Gordon 2017

The rights of Kay Barnham to be identified as the author and Mike Gordon as the illustrator of this Work have been asserted in accordance with the Copyright, Designs and Patents Act, 1988.

Managing editor: Victoria Brooker
Creative design: Paul Cherrill

feeling JEALOUS!

Written by
Kay Barnham

Illustrated by
Mike Gordon

free spirit
PUBLISHING®

"It's NOT fair," said Martha, punching a pillow.
"What's not fair?" Lucy asked. She was
Martha's best friend, and she was worried
about how upset Martha looked.

"Peter goes to bed at eight o'clock,"
huffed Martha, hurling a cuddly hippo
across the bedroom, "and I have
to go to bed at seven. See? *Not fair.*"
"Ah," said Lucy. She did see.

"Dad says I'm silly to feel jealous," added Martha. "He says that Peter's older than me, so of course he should go to bed later."

Lucy thought for a moment.
Then she smiled. If Martha could think of something good about being the younger one, then she might feel happier.

"Doesn't Peter have to unload the dishwasher?" asked Lucy.

"Yes," said Martha, looking puzzled.

"And does he take out the garbage, too?" Lucy went on.

"Er, yes," said Martha, beginning to smile. "Mom says he has to do more jobs because he's older…"

Lucy grinned. "Actually," said Martha with a giggle, "I don't like going to bed earlier than Peter, but I'm not at all jealous about his extra jobs."

At school the next day, Anthony was showing off his new hoverboard. "It's the best thing ever," he told anyone who would listen. "It's just like flying!"

"I wish he'd shut up about the stupid hoverboard," Anya muttered to Lucy.

"I want one really badly, but my mom says they're too expensive. It's not fair!"

Lucy wondered how she could help Anya look on the bright side. "Maybe you have a toy that Anthony doesn't have?" she suggested.

"I have a skateboard," Anya said,
kicking a stone. "It's kind of like a hoverboard.
I suppose I could play with that instead…"

"…while you're saving up,"
finished Lucy, with a wink.

A smile tugged at the corner of Anya's
mouth. It grew bigger and brighter
and Lucy couldn't help smiling back.

"I could, couldn't I?" Anya said.

"It would take a long, long time, but I could save up and buy my own hoverboard!"

After school, Lucy and her brother Alex went
to visit their Auntie Linda, who had just adopted
a scruffy old terrier named Bob.

"Bob is unbelievably cool," sighed Alex,
rubbing the dog behind the ears.
He loved animals so much.
He wanted to be a vet
when he grew up.

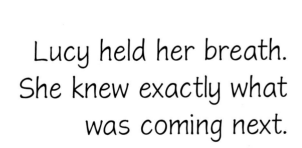

Lucy held her breath.
She knew exactly what
was coming next.

"I want a dog," said Alex. "Or a cat. Or a hamster. I'd even settle for a gerbil. I'd look after it really well. Why won't Mom and Dad let us have one?" he moaned.

"Erm...because Dad's allergic." Lucy said quietly.
Dad sneezed if he even looked at a furry animal.
Alex knew this, of course. But he still felt
jealous of everyone who had a pet.

"Auntie Linda," said Lucy, petting the little dog, "do you think we might be able to take Bob for walks? Could we sort of *share* him?"

"What a wonderful idea!" said Auntie Linda.
"Why don't we start now?"

And she handed Bob's leash to Alex,
who beamed with happiness.

The next week, it was the school sports day. Lucy was so excited. She would win every race for her team. Her friends' cheers would be
DEAFENING!

Even better, her parents were coming to watch Lucy and her brother take part.

They would be so proud!

But Lucy dropped her egg 27 times in the egg-and-spoon race.

In the sack race, she fell on her face.

In the hurdles race, there wasn't a single hurdle standing when she finished...in last place.

"Look, Alex is about to run the hurdles," Martha said to Lucy. "That'll cheer you up. Your brother's *so* fast."

Alex *was* fast. He was so fast that he finished in first place. Then he won the 100-meter race, too.

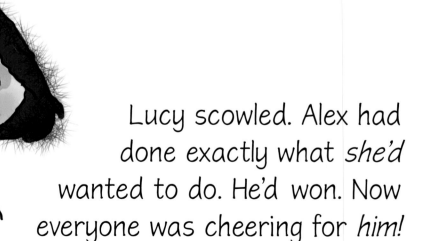

Lucy scowled. Alex had done exactly what *she'd* wanted to do. He'd won. Now everyone was cheering for *him!*

"Cheer up, Lucy," Martha said. "I know losing is hard, but the good thing is that your brother did so well."

Lucy saw Alex's shining face.
"I'll try to feel happy for him," she said.

"Besides, Alex is on the track team,"
Martha went on. "Why don't you take up a sport?
Then we could be cheering for *you* next year."
Lucy thought for a moment.
She did love swimming.

"Go on, have one of my medals," said Alex, hanging a medal around Lucy's neck. Lucy smiled at how everyone had bounced her own advice back at her.

And maybe it was good advice, because now she didn't feel jealous at all.

NOTES FOR PARENTS AND TEACHERS

The aim of this book is to help children think about their feelings in an enjoyable, interactive way. Encourage them to have fun pointing out details in the illustrations, making sound effects, and role playing. Here are more specific ideas for getting the most out of the book:

★ Encourage children to talk about their own feelings, if they feel comfortable doing so, either while you are reading the book or afterward. Here are a few conversation prompts to try:

  • When are some times you feel jealous? Why?

  • How do you stop feeling jealous at those times?

  • How do you think jealousy can affect the way people act toward each other?

  • This story shows many things that people might feel jealous about, such as toys, pets, and success. What other things can bring up jealous feelings?

★ Have children make face masks showing jealous expressions. Ask them to explain how these faces communicate jealousy.

★ Put on a feelings play! Ask groups of children to act out the different scenarios in the book. The children could use their face masks to show when they are jealous in the play.

★ Have kids make colorful word clouds. They can start by writing the word *jealous,* then add any related words or phrases they think of, such as *envy* or *I want that!* Have children write their words using different colored pens, making the most important words the biggest and less important words smaller.

★ Hold a jealous-face competition. Who can look the MOST jealous? Strictly no laughing allowed!

★ Green is a color that is often connected with jealousy and envy. In fact, jealousy is sometimes known as the green-eyed monster. Invite kids to draw or paint pictures of their own green-eyed monsters, making sure it looks super jealous! Then have children draw pictures of themselves taming the monsters and getting a handle on jealous feelings.

For even more ideas to use with this series, download the free Everyday Feelings Leader's Guide at www.freespirit.com/leader.

BOOKS TO SHARE

F Is for Feelings by Goldie Millar and Lisa A. Berger, illustrated by Hazel Mitchell (Free Spirit Publishing, 2014)

The Great Big Book of Feelings by Mary Hoffman, illustrated by Ros Asquith (Frances Lincoln, 2013)

Not Fair, Won't Share by Sue Graves, illustrated by Desideria Guicciardini (Free Spirit Publishing, 2014)

Peter's Chair by Ezra Jack Keats (Viking, 1998)

What to Do When It's Not Fair: A Kid's Guide to Handling Envy and Jealousy by Jacqueline B. Toner and Claire A. B. Thompson, illustrated by David Thompson (Magination Press, 2014)

When I Feel Jealous by Cornelia Maude Spelman, illustrated by Kathy Parkinson (Albert Whitman & Company, 2003)